WHO'S IN CHARGE HERE?

GERALD GARDNER

BERKLEY BOOKS, NEW YORK

For Harriet

NEW YORK, NEW YORK: WHO'S IN CHARGE HERE?

A Berkley Book / published by arrangement with the author

PRINTING HISTORY
Berkley edition / November 1981

ISBN: 0-425-05243-5

A BERKLEY BOOK® TM 757,375

PRINTED IN THE UNITED STATES OF AMERICA

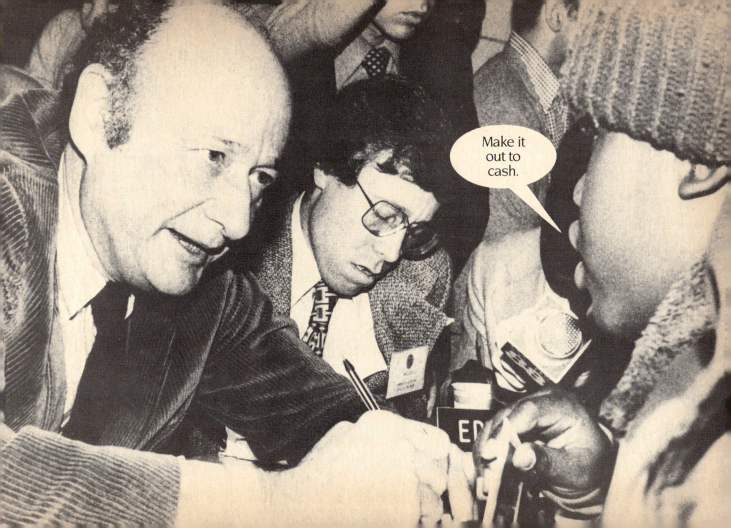

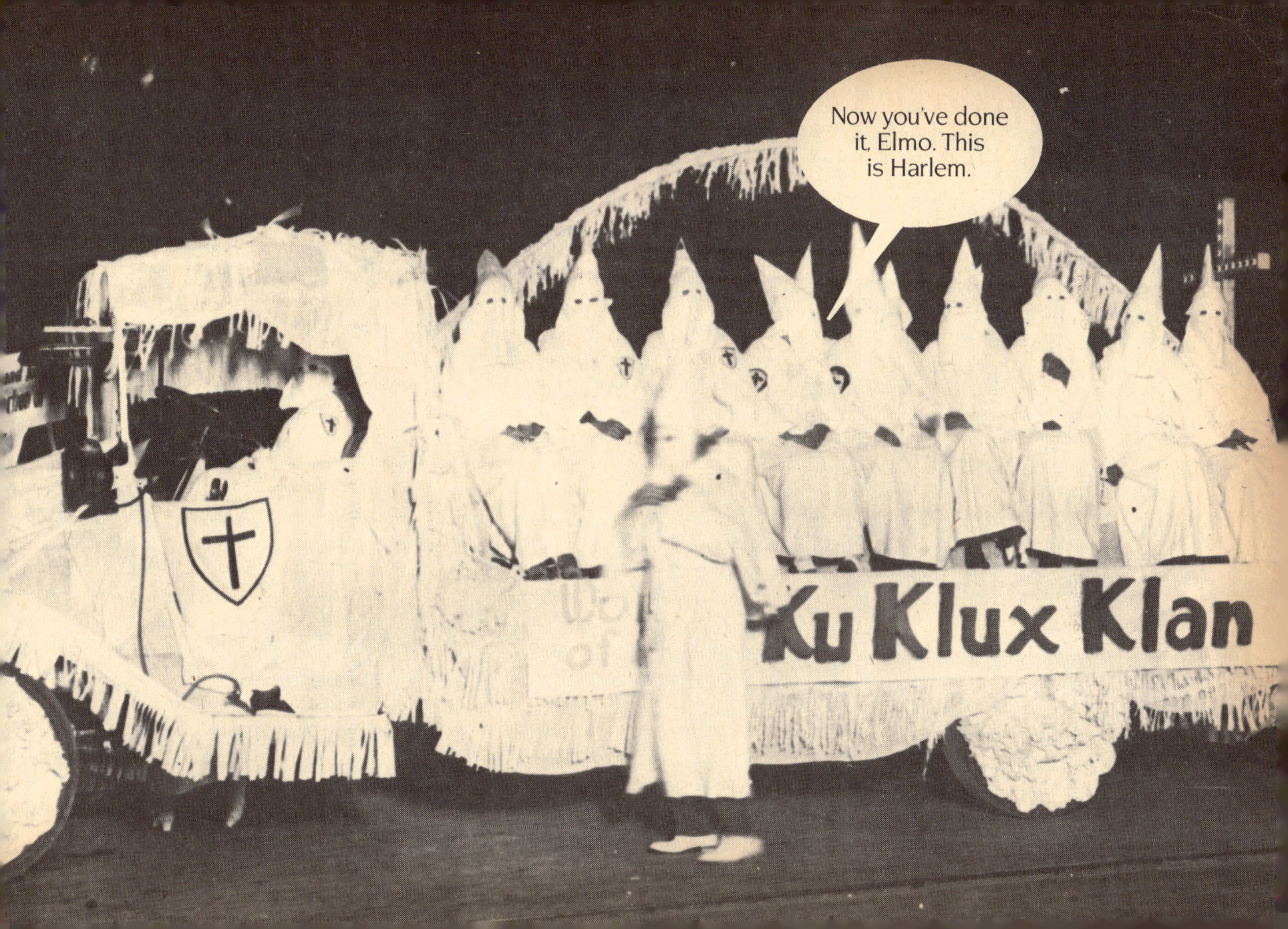
Now you've done it, Elmo. This is Harlem.
Ku Klux Klan

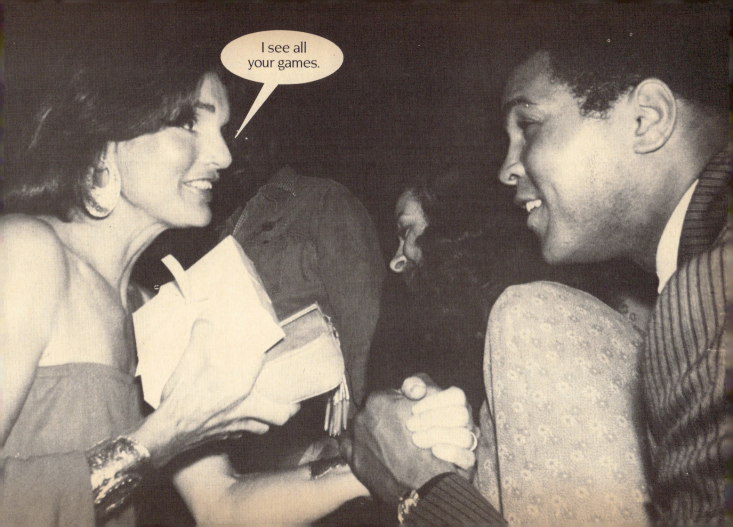

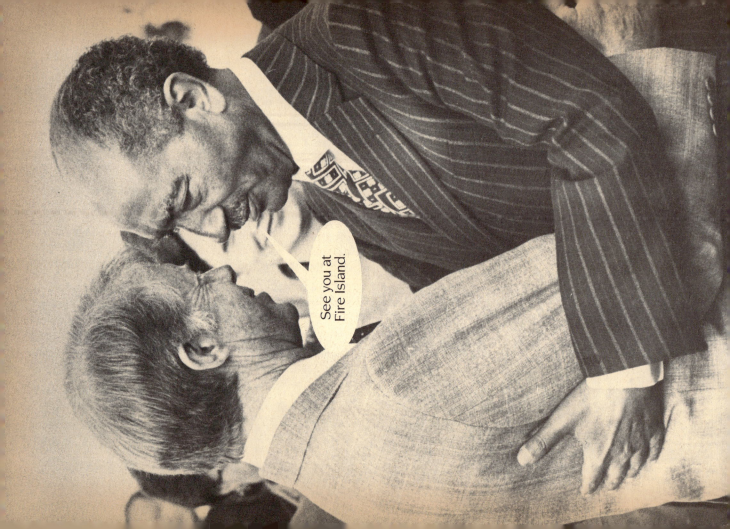

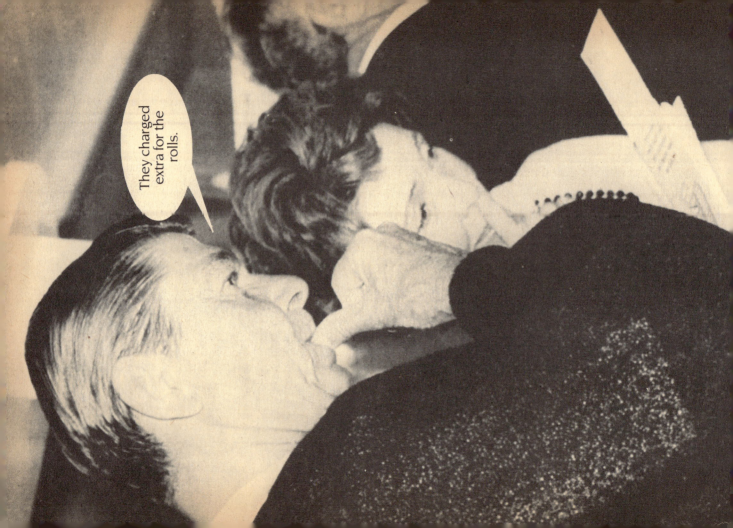

Why don't you just buy one?

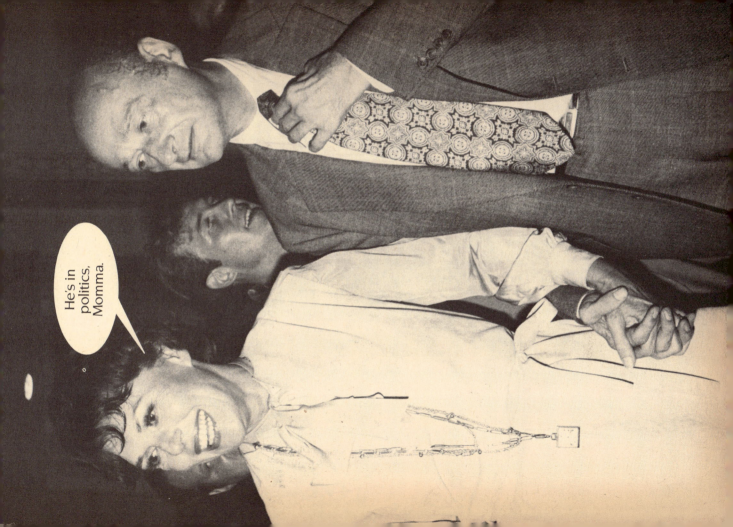

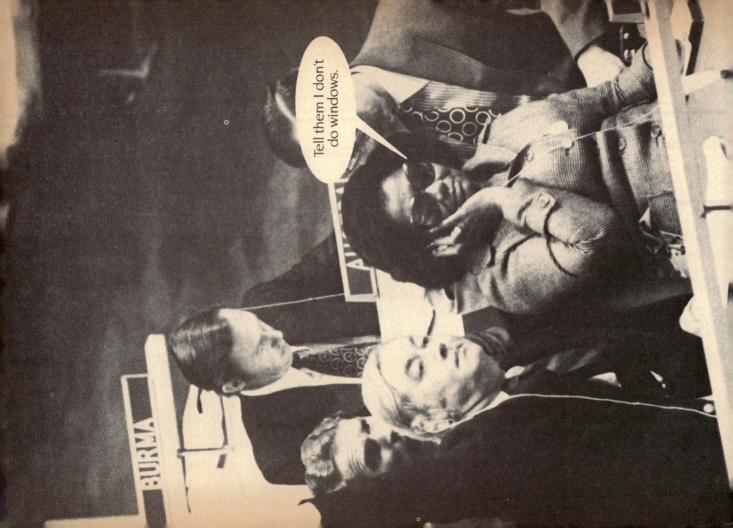

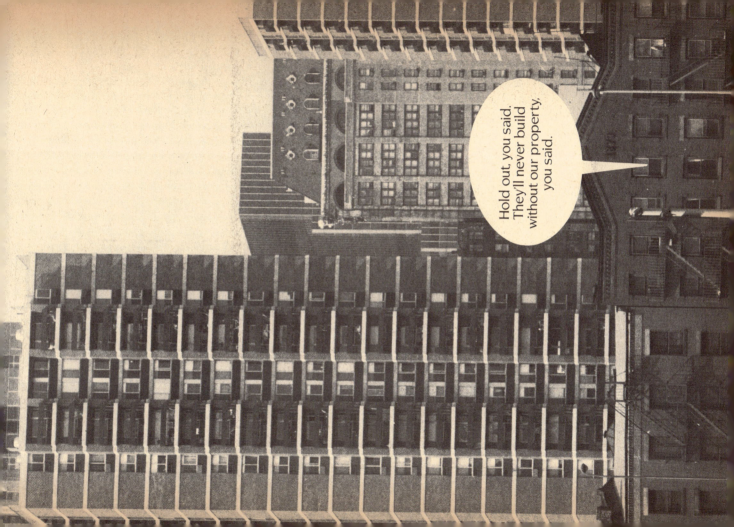

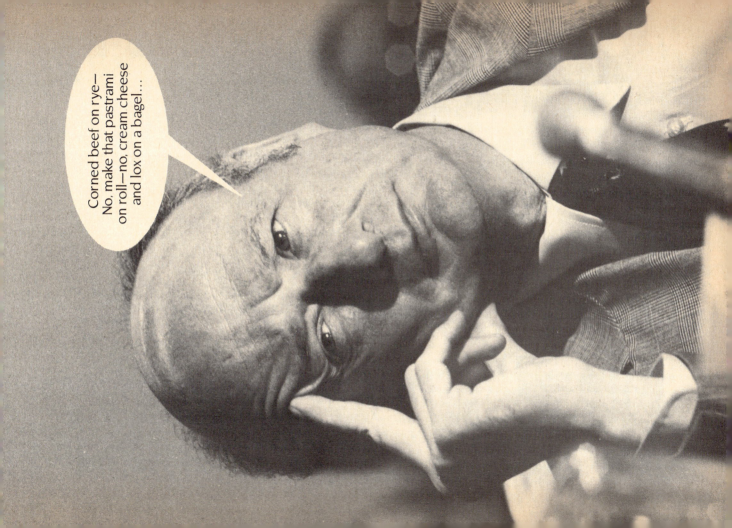

Welcome to The Dating Game.